Translated from the French by Claudia Zoe Bedrick

www.enchantedlion.com

First English-language edition published in 2019 by Enchanted Lion Books
67 West Street, 317A, Brooklyn, NY 11222
Copyright © 2019 for the English-language edition by Enchanted Lion Books
Text and illustrations copyright © Actes Sud Junior, 2016
First published in French as *La vie des mini-héros*
Book Layout & Design (US edition): Sarah Klinger
All rights reserved under International and Pan-American Copyright Conventions
A CIP record is on file with the Library of Congress. ISBN 978-1-59270-290-9

Printed in China by RR Donnelley Asia Printing Solutions Ltd.
1 3 5 7 9 10 8 6 4 2

LIFE AS A MINI HERO

OLIVIER TALLEC

ENCHANTED LION BOOKS

NEW YORK

This is for sure: Mini Heroes don't spend hours choosing what to wear every morning.

Mini Heroes are far too busy to ever get bored...

...except sometimes when it rains.

Mini Heroes aren't afraid of anything... at least not mini dogs.

Sometimes,
Mini Heroes are afraid of
the dark. But that's rare.

Occasionally, Mini Heroes have to stop being Mini Heroes...

...and be patient.

Mini Heroes don't always get to choose their missions.

But they must prevail nonetheless.

Mini Heroes have so many friends...

...they don't have time to pay attention to them all.

Mini Heroes often play pranks no one else laughs at.

But they don't like surprises very much themselves.

If there is one thing a Mini Hero hates...

...it's coming face-to-face with a rival.

Mini Heroes don't like impostors one bit.

Sometimes Mini Heroes need to be alone to think.

Mini Heroes love to be of service.

This is what distinguishes them.

Mini Heroes are sensitive to the weather.

Windy days are the worst.

They don't like when it's boiling hot either.

Sometimes Mini Heroes feel appreciated.

At other times, they have no doubt they are annoying everyone.

Mini Heroes never back down from a challenge.

Mini Heroes are surrounded by sidekicks
who help them triumph in their daily lives.

They have their preferences, of course.

Mini Heroes are adored by their friends.

They spend hours talking with them.

Mini Heroes are discreet and dislike show-offs.

Sometimes Mini Heroes feel different...

...even a little misunderstood.

Grown-ups often forget that Mini Heroes can be really slow because of the many traps they have to avoid, the number of rivers they have to cross, and the many buildings they have to climb.

Sometimes Mini Heroes wonder what would happen
if everyone in the world were a Mini Hero.